MAYAN
MURDER

MAYAN MURDER

Martha Brack Martin

orca soundings

ORCA BOOK PUBLISHERS

Library and Archives Canada Cataloguing in Publication

Martin, Martha, 1967–, author
Mayan murder / Martha Brack Martin.
(Orca soundings)

Issued in print and electronic formats.
ISBN 978-1-4598-1960-3 (softcover).—ISBN 978-1-4598-1958-0 (PDF).—
ISBN 978-1-4598-1959-7 (EPUB)

I. Title. II. Series: Orca soundings
PS8626.A77253M39 2018   JC813'.6   C2017-907690-6
                               C2017-907691-4

First published in the United States, 2018
Library of Congress Control Number: 2018933737

Summary: In this high-interest novel for teen readers, Tom and Kat
get caught up in a kidnapping while in Mexico on spring break.
A free teacher guide for this title is available at orcabook.com.

*Orca Book Publishers is dedicated to preserving the environment and has
printed this book on Forest Stewardship Council® certified paper.*

Orca Book Publishers gratefully acknowledges the support for its
publishing programs provided by the following agencies: the Government
of Canada through the Canada Book Fund and the Canada Council
for the Arts, and the Province of British Columbia through
the BC Arts Council and the Book Publishing Tax Credit.

Cover images by iStock.com/grandriver (front) and
Shutterstock.com/Krasovski Dmitri (back)

ORCA BOOK PUBLISHERS
orcabook.com

Printed and bound in Canada.

21 20 19 18 • 4 3 2 1

For Michael, Mac and Emma.
You will always be my favorite
companions—in travel and in life.

Chapter One

A spear sliced the air—an inch from my face!

I gasped for breath. I had to get off this path. But which way?

There was no time to think.

I threw myself to the right. The jungle swallowed me. Roots and branches became a wall trying to block me.

I tripped.

Another spear flew over my head. If I hadn't fallen, I'd be dead.

I looked up from the jungle floor.

The Mayan warrior was looming right over me. A new spear was aimed at my heart. There was no way he could miss.

His arm thrust downward. I braced myself for the feel of the wood piercing my chest.

Wait a minute. This all feels like a bad Indiana Jones *movie. I mean, how many spears can one guy carry?*

I woke up in a blood-pumping rush. My heart was racing like I really *was* fighting for my life in the Mexican jungle.

That's what I get for watching Apocalypto *on the plane.*

When I'd seen that a movie about the Maya was a choice on the flight, I'd gone for it. I thought I'd get a crash course on Mayan history. Instead, I'd fallen asleep and gotten a nightmare!

I checked the time. We'd be landing in Cancun in thirty minutes. This was my first flight anywhere, and I'd slept through most of it. Probably because I'd been too excited to sleep the night before. Having to get up at five in the morning hadn't helped either. I was so pumped to see Kat, it was a miracle I'd slept at all.

A whole week—spring break— with the super-smart, super-beautiful Kathleen Waters. In Mexico, no less. We'd only seen each other once since we met last September. A couple of days over Christmas holidays wasn't nearly enough. Thank god for cell phones and laptops. I couldn't wait to hang out with Kat in person for a whole week in the Riviera Maya. It was amazing that her dad had invited me to join them. Even more amazing that my dad had let me go. The plane ticket had been his birthday gift to me.

Now I just needed to relax and enjoy it.

When Kat and I first met, we'd been thrown into danger. We'd been lucky to survive. Ever since, I'd felt like I was always on high alert. Watching for trouble—and expecting to find it.

Take today at Detroit Airport. I kept bumping into this short guy in a red shirt. While I was checking in, going through security—even at the gate. It took me a while to realize we were probably on the same flight. So it was a no-brainer that we'd be in the same places. Still, there was something intense about him. Like the way he watched me as I walked up the aisle to my seat.

Give your head a shake, Tom. You've only got one job—to enjoy your first-ever tropical vacation with your fabulous girlfriend. Relax. Leave worrying about bad guys to Kat's dad. He's the FBI agent.

The pilot came on the PA to say we would be landing soon. That made me forget everything but Kat. Seven whole days. Bright blue water. A fancy all-inclusive resort. And Kat in a bikini. Paradise.

What could possibly go wrong?

Chapter Two

Kat was somewhere in the airport. It was torture waiting to get off the plane. I was behind three college guys who'd started their spring break early. They were drunk even though it was only about eleven AM Detroit time.

I finally lost them when I got off the plane. Kat was here last year, and she'd told me exactly where to go. I raced to the lower level.

The Immigration area was as nuts as Kat had said it would be. People were everywhere, filing into rows and rows of lineups like a maze. Instead of looking for the shortest line, I looked for Kat and her dad.

My phone dinged. A text from Kat. **R u here? We r far right**

I spotted Kat's dad, Mike, right away. Kat saw me coming and ran to meet me. I forgot all about the crowds (and her dad) when she gave me her usual Southern welcome. A hug to start. Then a kiss that made me really glad I'd popped gum during the landing. I could have kissed her all day, but she dragged me over to her dad.

"I see you made it, Tom," Mike said. He had a serious look on his face. I remembered that scary look from the first time we met. Then his face broke into a grin. He put out his hand to shake mine. "Great to see you again! Kathleen has been driving me crazy talking about you. Now she can finally stop!"

"Daddy!" Kat blushed. Then she just laughed. "He's right though. I have been talking about you a lot. I'm just so excited." I'd forgotten how much I loved her Southern accent. "This is going to be the best week ever!"

I grinned at her like an idiot. I couldn't help it. I turned to her dad. "Thanks again for inviting me, Mike." Mike waved away my thanks.

"How was your flight?" Kat asked. "Ours was late. We got in just before you. Did you have fun?"

"I tried to watch a movie, but I fell asleep." I spared her the details. "I was too excited to sleep last night."

Kat gave me a little squeeze. "Me too. There's so much I want to do this week!

Last year we stayed right in Cancun. It's all high-rises and traffic. Not like in the Mayan Riv. You can't snorkel off the beach in Cancun. And we only saw one ruin."

"Slow down and breathe, Kathleen." Mike looked at Kat with a raised eyebrow. "This is a holiday. I rented a car from the hotel, and yes, we'll do a few trips. But we're going to enjoy the resort too." We moved up farther in line. "This resort is supposed to be top of the line. There's lots to do there. And I am OFF DUTY. I want to snorkel. Lie by the pool and drink a *cerveza*—or three. Read my book and relax. I'm sure you and Tom can keep yourselves busy."

I could think of lots of ways Kat and I could keep busy. To distract myself from thinking too much about that, I scanned the airport walls. There was a giant poster with big gold letters announcing the *Rap in the Riv Fest*.

I knew some of the rappers listed. Big names. "We could go check that out," I said, pointing. "It's happening this week. Is Playa del Carmen nearby?"

Mike spoke before Kat could answer. "You aren't going anywhere near that. Not after what happened in January."

"What happened?" I asked.

"There was another big music festival in Playa, called the BPM. Big-name producers and artists from all over the world. With that kind of crowd, you get some serious drugs and crooks. One night it went bad. Five innocent people were killed."

"Now I remember. Didn't a drug cartel take credit?"

"Yeah, the Zetas hung up one of their 'banners.' But that wasn't all. The next day there was a shootout in Cancun. A group hit the office of a top lawyer working against the gangs. He survived. They got the gunmen."

"I thought the Mayan Riviera was supposed to be the safe part of Mexico. Aren't the drug cartels on the other side of the country?" I asked.

Mike shrugged. "For the most part you're right. The drug cartels are mainly based in the west. But lately there have been rumors that they're pushing into the Mayan." Mike moved forward in line. "Cancun's like any big city. There's always been some organized crime here. Where there's money, there's crime. Most of it you'd never know was going on. Tourists have usually been pretty safe here, as long as they weren't in the wrong place at the wrong time. Or doing something stupid."

We were almost at the front of the line. Finally.

"Things have been heating up lately," Kat added. "But the good guys are on it. Daddy's old training buddy, Jack, is the head investigator for all this recent stuff," Kat said. "He told him not to worry."

"I wouldn't have brought you kids down here if I thought it wasn't safe," Mike added. "Jack says they've got it under control." He pulled Kat into a hug. "And we're going to be regular tourists, enjoying our resort and staying out of trouble. But, sorry, no rap festival in Playa. There are shows each night at the resort. Even a disco, in case you want to get your moves on." Mike pretended to dance. Kat rolled her eyes.

It was finally our turn. We approached the immigration officer. Mike handed him his paperwork and Kat's. I slid mine over as the guy picked up Mike's.

Mike kept talking to Kat and me. "I'm just a regular tourist dad having a nice holiday with my kids," he said. "I don't want any drama."

The immigration guy at the booth was gesturing to someone behind us. Another guy came up. He was wearing a different uniform. One that came with a very big gun. He looked all business— and not good business. He took Mike's passport from the guy in the booth.

"Señor, you will have to come with me," the other guy said.

"Is there a problem?" Mike asked. Kat and I looked at each other.

"Not if you come with me now." The guy pointed at a side office. "Follow me, please. And bring your bag."

Mike turned to Kat and me. "You two finish up here. Then go get our suitcases. I'm sure this is nothing." He walked away.

So much for no drama.

The guy in the booth gave us back our passports. "Have a good stay," he said.

I wasn't so sure anymore.

But Kat grabbed my hand and gave me a big smile.

"We are going to have a *great* stay!" She leaned in and pulled me close. "We're together, and we're in paradise. It's going to be awesome."

Then she gave me a kiss that almost made me forget all about drug cartels and danger.

Almost.

Chapter Three

By the time Kat and I had grabbed our bags, Mike was back. I was about to ask him what they'd wanted. Then I saw his face.

"I could really use a beer," Mike said. "Let's get out of here."

I looked at Kat. She shrugged.

We walked through the rows of people selling time shares. Kat had warned me about them. They looked like travel agents and pretended to offer deals on trips. What they really wanted was to get you to listen to their sales pitch. I kept my eyes down and walked fast. Big glass doors led us into the sunshine.

The warm air and bright sun hit me. A big change from the winter I'd left behind. I stopped to take it all in.

Everything was lush and green. Trees in the parking lot were covered in flowers. They probably smelled amazing. I couldn't tell because of the diesel wafting from the waiting buses and vans. People were swarming like ants. A small group stood off to the side. Each person held a sign with someone's name on it.

Kat saw me looking at them. "Those are private drivers. For the VIPs and rich people."

Mike led us over to two short guys with matching shirts and clipboards. He gave them our names.

"These guys will take us to our resort. We'll pick up our rental car at the hotel. Easier than getting one here," Mike said. We climbed into a van while the driver loaded our bags.

When he came back, he offered Mike a beer—a *cerveza*—from his little cooler on the floor of the front seat. Mike took a big gulp. "Ahh...that hits the spot!" he said. The driver laughed as he pulled away.

As the van turned to leave the parking area, I spotted the guy in the red shirt again. I hadn't seen him since I'd boarded the plane. He walked out the glass doors and headed straight toward one of the private drivers. I tried to see the name on the driver's sign, but it was turned away from me.

Red Shirt was followed by a couple of guys with baggage carts loaded to the top with big black bags. The bags were different shapes—not suitcases either. Red Shirt looked up as our van went by. We locked eyes again with another one of those intense stares. We kept staring at each other until our van rounded the corner.

Red Shirt checked in when I did, back in Detroit. He didn't have all those bags then. So where did he get them? And what's inside?

"In about twenty minutes we'll be at our resort!" Kat's voice distracted me from my overactive imagination. She was almost bouncing up and down on the seat beside me. "This highway pretty much runs from Cancun all the way south. We'll know we're getting close when we see signs for Puerto Morelos. It's the closest town to our resort." She turned her guidebook to

18

show me. "It started as a little fishing village."

Mike chimed in. "It's supposed to be safe to walk there from the resort. But right now I'd feel better if you didn't go off on your own."

Kat was still reading the guidebook. "You can hire local tour guides in town to take you snorkeling on the reef. We are definitely doing that. The reef is the second-longest barrier reef in the world. It's why tourists started coming to the Mayan area."

"We can get a ride out to the reef at the resort too, Kathleen." Mike turned to me. "The resort has its own marina."

I had to laugh. "I go on vacation and *still* end up at a marina!" I said.

"I'd rather go from town with the local guides, Daddy. Prices are probably cheaper, and we want to check out the town anyway." Kat turned to me, raising an eyebrow. "Though I have to say marinas *are* pretty awesome. We wouldn't have met if you didn't have one."

"True." I grinned.

"We're almost there," Mike said, pointing as we passed a sign for Puerto Morelos. There was one for our resort right beside it.

We turned off the highway. The resort had its own laneway. Both sides were lined with crazy twisty-rooted bush-type things sitting in water. Kat saw me looking.

"Those are mangroves. Nature's nursery for baby birds, fish—even alligators," Kat explained. "The resort is eco-friendly. They had to get permission to build here. It's a protected area."

The mangroves opened to a big fancy entrance with flags flying. We unloaded fast and went to check in. In minutes we were handed pretty drinks, room keys and plastic bracelets. Kat's and mine were white. Mike's was bright orange.

"Don't lose these bracelets," the front-desk lady told us. "They prove you're guests at the resort." She called over the bellhop and gave him our room number.

"And no booze," Mike added. "Your bracelet shows you're underage, so you won't be served any alcohol. Some resorts don't pay attention. But this one does." His pulled us aside and lowered his voice. "I want you to promise me that you two will make smart choices. I know spring break is a thing, and you're teens. But there've been some crazy news reports latcly. Part of what we were talking about earlier. Stories of tourists drinking only a few drinks, then blacking out. People being drugged at resorts. Kids your age even." He looked me in the eye, then Kat. "I'm serious. One young girl died."

"Well, thanks for that happy start to our vacation, Daddy," Kat said.

She turned to me. "This is what happens when your dad is FBI. You hear all the horrible stuff." She cut Mike off as he started talking again. "Okay, okay. We promise we'll be safe and danger free. Now no more doom and gloom." She grabbed my hand. "Let's go check out our suite."

Mike led us to a golf cart that already had our bags loaded. The bellhop drove quickly, dodging guests walking up the paths. In no time we were walking into our suite. I felt my jaw drop, but I couldn't help it.

The place was almost as big as my whole house! There was a bedroom with two beds and a massive, fancy bathroom. Mike and Kat were sharing that. There was also another bathroom and a living room with an eating area. The guy showed us how to pull a big bed out of the wall. That was for me. Both the living room and bedroom had sliding glass doors to the balcony. I stepped out to get a better look at the Gulf of Mexico sparkling in the sun. I'd never seen water that blue.

"What do you think, Tom?" Mike was grinning from ear to ear. "Pretty nice, eh?"

"It's *incredible*," I said. "Thanks again for letting me come."

"We're glad to have you." Mike looked like he meant it. "Now let's get unpacked and get out there!"

Chapter Four

We headed to the pool. It was mid-afternoon, so most of the loungers were taken. Kat and I managed to find two together. Mike grabbed a single under an umbrella.

"You kids go have fun. Don't worry about me. I just want to lie here and have me some mojitos." Mike called over the pool server. Kat wouldn't leave her dad until she'd slathered his bald head with sunscreen.

I'd called my dad earlier to tell him I'd made it here safe and sound. He'd made me promise to use sunscreen too. I dug it out.

"I can put that on for you," Kat offered. I pictured Kat rubbing lotion all over me. I'd need a cold shower before she was through.

"I'm good." I put on the sunscreen fast. "I just want to get into that pool. It looks amazing."

The resort had a jumping cliff in the pool. We took turns making crazy poses as we jumped. The water felt great. Before long Mike was napping. The two empty mojito glasses might have had something to do with that.

"Let's grab a soda," Kat said. "I've missed just hanging out with you."

"I've missed it too."

The swim-up bar was packed. The bartenders poured and mixed drinks faster than my eye could follow. The people were fun to watch too. Drunk, loud or crazy—and sometimes all three.

A number of people in blue resort uniforms were moving around the pool area. They seemed to be rounding up guests for something. I didn't care what. I just wanted Kat to myself. We found a spot away from the crowd, where it was more private.

Kissing Kat is always incredible. But kissing Kat under the Mexican sun, with the smell of salt water on the breeze? That was a whole new level of awesome.

It took me a second to realize Kat was pulling back. A shadow stood over us. I was dimly aware that someone was tapping Kat on the shoulder. Then I noticed the blue resort uniform.

Do they have a rule about kissing in public?

"Señorita! My name is Pedro! I am part of the animation team at the resort." He pointed proudly at his uniform. "Come and play the water polo with us. We need a beautiful girl on our team!"

I couldn't believe this guy! Some nerve, interrupting us. I was just about ready to tell Pedro where he could go when Kat said, "Let's play!" Then she saw my face. "Oh, come on! It'll be fun. We have lots of time for us later."

I didn't want to be a jerk, but I was mad. There was no way I was playing water polo. Even whipping the ball hard at Pedro wouldn't make me feel better.

"You go if you want. I'll watch."

"You sure? Don't be mad. I'll make it up to you later." Kat lifted one eyebrow in that way I loved. "Daddy's headed over here anyway." She pointed at Mike.

"Okay. But see if you can hit Pedro in the head for me, eh?" I said. Kat laughed.

Mike was carrying all his stuff. "I've had enough sun for the first day. I'm going back to the suite."

"We'll join you when she's done," I told him. We watched Kat score a goal.

"Did you see that, Daddy?" she yelled. Mike nodded, gave her a thumbs-up and then headed off.

A lady was standing near me in the pool. "Your friend is a real beauty. She sounds like she's from the South, like me. My name's Alex. Where are y'all from?"

I had to remind myself not to be suspicious. *Don't freak out. She's just being friendly.*

"I'm from Canada. My friend and her dad are from Virginia."

"I thought so!" Alex was nodding. "I'm from Virginia too. Lynchburg. I'm a high-school history teacher. What part of Virginia are your friends from?"

Because of Mike's job, I didn't think I should answer that. "I forget. But my friend"—I pointed at Kat—"is crazy about history. You guys will have to talk."

Right then Kat swam over to me. "You should have played with us!" She splashed me.

"Kat, this is Alex. She teaches history in Lynchburg."

"Well then, Alex, you should join us for dinner," Kat said with a big smile. "If you're here with friends, bring them too."

I looked at Kat like she was crazy. It was our first night here, and Mike had said he wanted to relax, not meet strangers.

"I'm here on my own. My friend had to cancel at the last minute. I decided to come anyway." She laughed. "Teaching high school is scarier than traveling alone!"

"You should join us for sure then. Want to meet at the buffet around six?"

"Well, thank you. That sounds great. This is my second day, and I haven't met many people."

"It'll be fun. I'm sure my daddy, whose name is Mike, would love to have some grown-up company," Kat said.

I wasn't so sure.

As we walked off, Kat whispered in my ear, "She's perfect for Daddy! She's pretty and smart—and she's from Virginia!"

"Were we supposed to be finding Mike a date?"

"Daddy's lonely. It's been years since Mama died. And Alex seems great!" Kat almost squealed. "Daddy will be thrilled."

"I hope you're right. Because I don't want to see Mad Mike again. Mad Mike is scary."

"Trust me. He'll like her. Plus..." Kat took my hand. She pulled me toward her. "If Daddy is busy with Alex"— she paused, her lips an inch away from mine—"that means we can have more time alone."

"Unless there's a water-polo game."

"Stop being a baby." She closed the space between us with her lips. My mind filled with ideas of all the ways we could spend that alone time.

"I love how you think," I said.

Chapter Five

Kat told Mike about Alex when we got back to the room. He took it better than I'd expected he would. He said he was too tired to be charming, but he did put on a nice shirt.

"You'll like her, Daddy. And she's all by herself on this trip. I couldn't let her eat alone." Kat fixed Mike's collar.

"You look great. Come on. We'll have fun."

We headed out. On the main path some locals had set up little stalls full of all kinds of local crafts and trinkets.

"Oh. Let's shop!" Kat squealed.

"After dinner. Our guest is waiting, remember?" Mike steered Kat away.

We made our way to the buffet. There were special restaurants at the resort too, but you had to book them ahead of time.

I was expecting something like my high-school cafeteria, but I was blown away by the spread.

"There's every kind of food here I can think of! How do I pick?" I asked Kat.

She laughed and grabbed some sushi. "Try a little of everything. You can come back as many times as you want."

"This really is paradise," I said.

Dinner was fun. Mike and Alex hit it off like old friends. It was weird to see Mike relaxed and…well…normal. I could tell Kat was thrilled.

After dinner we checked out the stalls. Alex and Kat looked at silver stuff. I looked for things I could bring back for my friend Nate and my dad. Mike walked ahead.

After a minute, I looked up and noticed Mike off to the side, talking quietly with one of the sellers. He looked intense. Clearly FBI Mike was back. My eyes scanned the shoppers for Kat.

She was heading my way. Alex was nowhere to be seen.

"Check out your dad," I said, pointing. "What do you think that's about?"

"Maybe he's asking for tour ideas?" Kat tried to joke, but I knew she could see her dad was back in FBI mode too.

Mike saw us. He stopped talking and walked toward us.

"What's going on?" Kat asked. "You're up to something."

"I was just shopping." Mike tried to put us off.

"Nice try. You were getting intel from that guy," Kat said.

Mike sighed. "I was just trying to get a feel for things. How safe it is. What the word is from the locals." He waved at Alex, who had come into view. "Now drop it. Here comes Alex."

"The fire show is about to start by the pool," she said. "Do y'all want to stay and watch?"

It sounded good, so we grabbed drinks and found seats. The dancers were dressed like the Mayans in my dream. But instead of spears, they tossed fire. The drums, the flames—it was amazing! When it was over I realized I'd been holding my breath the whole time.

"I think I need a nightcap at the beach bar," Alex said. "Anyone care to join me?"

"I'm too tired," Kat said. "And Tom and I are getting up early to see the sun rise."

We are? So much for sleeping in.

"I'm afraid I'll have to take a rain check too, Alex. This has been one hell of a long day. A great day—don't get me wrong. But I'm ready for bed," Mike said.

"Well, maybe I'll see y'all tomorrow?" Alex looked hopeful.

"For sure!" Kat said. "Sleep well."

We walked back to our suite. Mike headed straight to bed.

"Let's check out the stars from the balcony," Kat said.

The moon was a big ball of silver. I was used to seeing it hover over the river at home. But here it looked bigger. Brighter. Stars dotted the sky. Kat and

I lay beside each other on the balcony hammock. The music from the beach bar drifted up. It was perfect.

Kat was perfect.

We started picking up where we'd left off in the pool. Then I remembered we weren't alone.

"Your dad's in the next room," I reminded Kat.

"He's probably asleep by now," Kat said.

As if on cue, Mike's voice rang out from the bedroom.

"I left my balcony door open so I could hear the waves," he said. "And I'm still wide awake."

What did he hear? Could he see us?

Kat started laughing. Then I started laughing too.

"Thanks for the heads-up, Daddy!" Kat said.

"Well, since you two plan to be up for the sunrise," Mike went on, "you might want to get to bed now." He paused. "And by that I mean...right now!"

When your girlfriend's dad is a protective, six-foot-four-inch FBI agent, romance is a real challenge.

"Yes, Daddy." Kat gave me a quick kiss. "See you bright and early!"

Bright and early.

Ugh.

Chapter Six

"Tom. *Tom*. Wake up!" I'd been dreaming about Kat. It took me a minute to figure out she was really there. "Come on. We're going to miss the sunrise."

I was so tired, I wasn't sure I could open my eyes.

Somehow I managed to pull myself out of bed and get to the beach.

Kat took a ton of pictures while I walked around like a zombie. A few other people were around. Workers cleaned up from the night before. Guys raked the beach. Two guests were putting towels on chairs.

"We need to claim some chairs too. Here," Kat said, handing me her camera. She had brought towels with her. I'd missed that. She picked three loungers by the pool. "They call this the towel game," she said. She tucked our towels into the chairs. She topped one with a blue floppy hat. "That's how we can tell they're ours."

"Great. Any chance we can go back to bed now?"

"Sure can. We're all set."

We headed back to the room. In seconds I was dreaming again.

My second start to the day was much better. It involved a hot shower and a buffet breakfast. I wished Dad was here to see the mountains of bacon. I pigged out.

"Let's check out the rest of the resort," Kat said. "You can start walking off some of that bacon! And we can sign up for that bike tour into town."

"I need to go to the marina," Mike said. "I want to ask about fishing and snorkeling trips." Kat opened her mouth. He cut her off. "I know you want us to contact the local tour guides in town. But it won't hurt to ask. You can probably sign up for the bike tour there too. Why don't you come with me?"

The marina was farther up the beach, at the very end of the resort.

"Holy cow. Dad would kill for this," I said when we got closer. It was beyond impressive.

In the marina office, maps and posters of the Mayan coast were all over the walls. Mike talked to an older man at the back while Kat and I looked around.

"Can I help you?" a young guy asked as he walked into the office. He was wearing a white T-shirt with the resort logo on it. He looked about twenty.

"We're just waiting for my dad," Kat said. "My name's Kat. This is Tom." I smiled a hello. "We want to sign up for today's bike tour into town. Can we do that here?"

"You can. Let me just put it into the computer." He kept talking as he typed. "My name is Antonio. And you are all set for the tour. You need to meet in the lobby in thirty minutes."

"We'd also like to snorkel the reef. But I think we're going to do that from town. My father is just checking your prices," Kat said, pointing at Mike.

"Well, the reef is great for sure, however you get there. But if you want to see our sea turtles, you should also plan to visit Akumal. It is a protected place for them. You can snorkel right off the beach."

Mike was finished talking to the older guy, who introduced himself as the marina boss. "Ready to go, kids?" he asked.

Kat nodded and turned to Antonio. "We'd love to come back again later, if that's okay? Tom's family owns a marina. You two could probably talk for hours."

"Our marina can't compare to this one," I said. "We're small. On the Detroit River. The Canadian side."

"I would love to hear more about your marina and your river. And I will tell you more about Akumal," said Antonio. "I am very interested in marine biology. I want to study it in university. But first I need to make enough money."

We said goodbye and made our way back to the lobby. It turned out Pedro was leading the tour. *Great*. Kat laughed when she saw my face.

The town of Puerto Morelos was cool. Pedro pointed out the main sights. Then we had an hour to do our own thing. Kat wanted to visit a bookstore called Alma Libre. She bought some more guidebooks while I waited outside.

All around the town square were posters for the Rap in the Riv Fest. I was reading one when a cab pulled up. A woman stepped out. She spoke rapid-fire Spanish to the driver. When she turned I saw that it was Alex.

There is nothing weird about this, I reminded myself. People take cabs.

Kat came out of the store. "The pier where we can book a guide and boat is right there," she said.

I pointed out Alex, and Kat called her over.

Alex looked happy to see us. She was in town to book a snorkeling trip too.

Then she was going to do a little shopping, she said.

"Perfect!" Kat said. "You can come snorkeling on our boat with us."

"I don't want to crash your party. I can join some other group."

"Don't be silly." Before I knew it, Kat had booked a trip for all four of us for the next morning. Our captain had two gold teeth right in the middle of his smile. His name was equally cool.

"I am called Crispy Bacon," he said. I couldn't wait to tell Dad. He'd love that.

It was almost time to rejoin the bike tour. Kat bugged Alex until she agreed to join us for dinner. We were planning to try the Japanese restaurant.

We biked back to the resort quickly. We grabbed a bite at the snack bar by the pool and found Mike. He didn't look surprised to hear that Kat had booked our tour. And he seemed fine with

Alex joining us for dinner and the trip. I sat beside him in the shade while Kat grabbed a pool float. She wanted to "get her tan on."

Mike and I looked over at a group of college girls at the swim-up bar. "People-watching is part of the fun down here," Mike said. The girls had clearly already done a bunch of shots. Now they were holding one of those pink lawn flamingos upside down like a funnel, calling it a "flabongo."

"Why would they even bother?" I asked.

Mike shrugged. "Who knows." He smiled. "Kids do stupid things." He turned to me, his face suddenly serious. "That's why it's so important to be careful. I'm glad you always have your eyes open, Tom. Bad guys can show up anywhere. Sometimes where you least expect them. That's why we need good guys." He paused.

"That reminds me. I need to call my old buddy Jack. Hopefully he's not too busy to meet us. With this rap fest, he's probably up to his eyeballs in crazy."

Mike got up and grabbed his phone and towel. "Tell Kathleen she needs more sunscreen," he said before he walked away.

Chapter Seven

Dinner at the Japanese restaurant was very cool. The chef cooked right in front of us. It was more a show than a meal. At one point he shot a piece of fried egg at me. I caught it in my mouth, and everyone cheered.

"I see you have some untapped skills," Kat said.

"You have no idea," I said.

We were eating our main course when Mike turned to Alex.

"The kids and I are going to snorkel off the beach at Akumal on Wednesday morning—hopefully spot some sea turtles. Any chance you'd want to join us?"

Kat squeezed my leg.

"I think I've imposed on y'all enough. You're already taking me snorkeling tomorrow," Alex said.

"We'd love to have you," Kat added. "The more the merrier."

"We can all go in the rental car. I was hoping to get an early start. My friend said it gets pretty crowded later in the day."

Kat was looking at her food with a big smile on her face. I knew that look. It had nothing to do with her food.

I whispered, "Okay, you win. Mike is totally going for Alex."

"Don't jinx it," Kat whispered back. She turned to Mike. "Didn't you say you'd made plans to meet Jack for lunch that day too?"

"Yes, he has a meeting there. He suggested we eat at a little place called La Buena Vida. Jack says the view is great and the food is even better."

"Well then, I'm in," Alex said. "I can't pass up great food or a great view. But I'm going to have to invite y'all over to my place once we get back home. I owe you a few meals."

Mike didn't answer right away. I jumped in to change the topic.

"So how do you and Jack know each other again?" I asked Mike.

"We took a course together a few years ago. Jack is in law enforcement here," Mike said. "They sent him to Virginia for leadership training. We had a lot of laughs. Managed to get in some great golf too. His real name is Joaquin. He grew up in Cancun. Now he's in charge of their biggest cases."

Mike took a sip of his mojito. "It'll be great to see him again."

After dinner we all headed to the resort's theater to catch the comedy show. It wasn't Broadway. But it was okay.

"How about a drink at the beach bar?" Alex asked. "You can't turn me down two nights in a row."

"Sure. What about you kids?" Mike asked.

Kat gave my leg another squeeze. "I think I'm too tired," she said. "All that bike riding in the sun. And we were up early."

I chimed in, "Yeah, I'm ready for bed. You two go ahead."

Mike gave Kat a look and then turned to Alex. "I guess it's just the two of us." He didn't look like he minded.

They walked off, and Kat and I headed back to our suite. I was already remembering the night before. Balcony.

Martha Brack Martin

Moon. And this time no Mike in the room next door.

"I need to give you your birthday present," Kat said. My mind was still on the previous night. I was almost sad when I saw a box in her hand.

"Oh! Right!" I fumbled for words. "I mean, thanks. You didn't have to. It's enough of a present that I'm here with you."

We sat on the couch, and I unwrapped the box. Inside was a high-tech watch. A real beauty I could never have afforded myself.

"It's a Pyle Sports Snorkeling Master. For diving and snorkeling," Kat said excitedly. "It can tell you everything. Water temperature. Depth. And it's totally waterproof."

"I love it."

"I figured with the marina, you needed a really good waterproof watch.

And this way you can always remember our trip."

"It's amazing," I said. She helped me put it on. I closed the distance between us. "And so are you."

I started showing her just how amazing I thought she was.

Boom, boom, boom!

We both jumped at the sound of the pounding on the suite door. It took me a moment to breathe again.

I got up. As I grabbed the knob, it turned in my hand.

"Hi, kids!" Mike said with a big grin on his face. He walked into the room. "Did you like my knock? I had my key. But I didn't want to *scare* you by just walking in."

Yeah. Like that knock wasn't scary at all.

"Daddd-ddy!" Kat made the word last. "You scared us half to death!"

Mike's grin got even wider. "Well, now that I'm here, you don't need to be scared. And that's good. Because I remember how tired you both are. *So* tired you couldn't join Alex and me."

There was no way he'd missed what Kat was up to earlier.

"And since we're *all* so tired, I guess we should *all* get to bed right now." He opened his bedroom door. "Let's go, my girl. Good night, Tom."

Kat followed her dad into the room. She blew me a kiss behind his back.

"Goodnight," I said.

Paradise was great. But it was also very frustrating.

Chapter Eight

"My friends, we are going to see the big fish today!" Crispy Bacon's gold teeth sparkled in the morning sun. "You have the best guide—my son Juan. And, of course, you have the best captain. Crispy Bacon!" He smacked his chest and laughed.

The boat was heading straight to the reef. I looked back to see the pier shrinking behind us. The boat smelled like home. Gas and oil, with a tang of fish.

"This is going to be amazing!" Kat said. It was just the four of us. The water was a little rough, but Crispy said we'd be okay.

The area was spotted with buoys and boats. Crispy anchored us at a red buoy. "We must use the buoys to protect the reef. Do not touch the coral with your fins. And stay with your guide." He went through more safety rules. Then he brought out our gear.

"Daddy has his own special mask. He bought it just for this trip," Kat told Alex and me.

Mike pulled it out of his snorkel bag. "It's supposed to be top of the line." He was excited. "Mask and snorkel in one. Covers my whole face." He put it on. "How do I look?"

We all tried not to laugh.

"It's great, Daddy. Especially with your big bald head. Now get over here and let me get some sunscreen on you." Kat slathered him up.

The rest of us grabbed gear from Crispy. His son showed us the right way to "fall" off a snorkeling boat into the water. Then we were off.

I'd snorkeled lots of times at home, mostly to look for stuff people had dropped from their boats accidentally, or to fix things. Snorkeling on a tropical reef was nothing like that. For one thing, the water was bright and sparkling, not dark and gloomy like the water in the Detroit River. And everywhere I looked, something was moving. Schools of little fish in every color. Big silver fish as wide as me. Purple coral waving back and forth like fans. I wished Dad was with me. He'd loved this.

Kat spotted a big stingray at the same time as our guide pointed it out.

It was huge. We knew enough to keep our distance. Watching it swim was incredible. Then our guide made a hand sign. Time to head back to the boat.

When we were all on board, Crispy moved us to a second spot on the reef. "Let's see if we can find you some turtles," he said.

"Hey, how did your watch work?" Kat asked.

"Great. Apparently, the water was seventy-nine degrees!" I grinned.

We didn't see any turtles at the second spot, but we did see a massive barracuda. Its teeth were scary.

The water was getting rougher, and it was hard to swim. We were all ready for shore when our guide took us back to the boat.

Mike looked a little green. "It's because you are such a big man, Señor," Crispy said. "You have to work harder in the water."

"It also might be the two omelets you ate for breakfast," Kat said.

"Don't mention them," Mike muttered, "unless you want to see them again."

Even though Mike felt sick by the end of our excursion, we all agreed that we'd had a great time. After we got back to shore and unloaded our gear, Kat said she wanted to do a little shopping. Mike decided to take a pass and sat in the town square.

Alex was a big help. Kat's Spanish was good, but Alex spoke like a local. She got me a great deal on a mask for my buddy Nate and a leather wallet for Dad. Kat picked up a bunch of things, but her big purchase was a handmade leather whip.

"Only my kid would buy a whip!" Mike laughed when we met up with him again. He was looking less green.

"It's a work of art. Look at it!" Kat said. "I'm going to hang it above my bed."

I shook my head. "Did you always want to be Indiana Jones?" I asked.

"Absolutely. Why do you think I love history so much?" Kat grinned.

We grabbed lunch back at the resort. Mike didn't feel like eating and went to nap in the room. Alex said she had some work to do, but she ate with us before she took off.

"Is it weird that Alex has work to do?" I asked. "Like, it's spring break in Mexico." I didn't want to be suspicious. But I still couldn't shake the feeling that I needed to be on high alert.

"I think she didn't want to keep hanging out with us without Dad."

"Yeah, I guess. But is it weird that she speaks Spanish like a local? I mean, she's from Virginia."

"That brain is always working, isn't it?" Kat laughed. "Don't forget that Spanish is our country's second language.

And she's traveled a lot." She shrugged. "I think it's great. And I think *she's* great. Daddy likes her. So relax!"

"It's my stupid radar. I can't stop looking for trouble."

"Well, we aren't going to find any here. We're in paradise." Kat shook her head at me. "And since we didn't see any turtles today, let's go talk to Antonio. Maybe he can tell us where we have the best chance of finding some in Akumal tomorrow," Kat said.

Antonio was happy to see us. He was also happy to tell us more about Akumal. We toured the marina while we talked. I recognized some of the boats. Most would never be in our marina. Way too fancy.

"My grandfather has been a fisherman in Akumal his whole life. You should look for his boat when you go. She's bright green and is called *The Thirsty Turtle*.

My uncles are fishermen too. But *Abuelo*—that's 'grandfather' in Spanish— he's the boss. He knows everyone and everything in Akumal."

"Your dad doesn't fish?" Kat asked.

"No. My parents are teachers. My mother came here from New York to improve her Spanish. She got a job teaching English in a school here. That's where she met my father. And now… here I am."

"That's why your English is so good," I said.

"*Gracias*. It helped me get this job. I need to make good money. University is not cheap," he said. "Anyway, Akumal is the best place for turtles. But don't listen to the men trying to sell you tours. They will say you need a guide to swim with the turtles. But they lie."

He showed us a map. "Stay away from here." He pointed. "There has been trouble lately. Fighting and roadblocks."

I looked at Kat. More trouble in paradise. Was this part of whatever was going on?

"Why is there trouble?" Kat asked.

"The fake guides bring many tour buses in. They don't follow rules. Too many people and bad sunscreen." He shook his head. "The Centro Ecologico Akumal protects the turtles. Some of them are getting cancer, probably from the sunscreens. They are stressed from too many people swimming in their habitat." Antonio looked angry. "The Centro asked the government to stop these unlicensed buses from entering. But someone with money is helping these guides. Telling them to fight."

"They aren't with a real tour company?" I asked.

"No." Antonio's voice got quiet. "There are lots of strangers coming into the Mayan lately. Bad groups from the west."

"We heard about the drug cartels pushing into the area."

"Yes. They want to take over. And tourism is a good way to clean dirty money."

Antonio's boss called to him from the office.

"I better go. But here—take my cell number." He quickly wrote it on a paper from his pocket. "Call me if you need directions or run into trouble." He smiled. "And if you see *The Thirsty Turtle*, say hi to Abuelo for me."

"We will. Thanks, Antonio!" Kat turned to me. "I wonder if the cartels are really the ones behind the shady tour guides. It could be someone local. I bet Jack knows."

"Yeah. And maybe my radar's not so stupid after all. It sounds like we're right to keep our eyes open." I thought of what Mike had said to me at the pool, about bad guys being everywhere.

"This place is definitely paradise…"
I paused. "But even paradise had
a snake."

Chapter Nine

Our morning snorkel off Akumal beach was amazing. We saw the tour guys Antonio had told us about, but we ignored them.

Kat and I snorkeled together and left Mike and Alex to do their own thing. At first we didn't see much. Just little tufts of seagrass sprouting from the sandy bottom. Then—out of nowhere—a huge turtle loomed up in front of us. It was at least two and a half feet wide. Two smaller ones were right behind it. They were beautiful. Unreal. They dove down and nibbled the grass sprouts. They didn't care that we watched them. It was wild.

Afterward we met up with Mike and Alex and walked along the beach. Brightly painted boats lined the shore, but we didn't see *The Thirsty Turtle.* Abuelo was probably out fishing.

Two big buses full of tourists arrived as we returned to the rental car. If you didn't know any better, you'd think they were legit.

La Buena Vida was a quick drive up the bay. Jack wasn't there yet. We sat right on the beach, taking in the view. The waiter said there had been a manatee swimming out front earlier.

"I feel like I understand Aquaman a lot better now that I've seen real sea turtles," Mike said. "No wonder he could ride them. They're huge."

"Daddy, you are so weird." Kat shook her head.

Alex ordered four margaritas. "The kids should try an authentic margarita at least once, don't you think, Mike?"

Kat and I were shocked when Mike agreed.

"What happened to the 'no booze in the Mayan' rule?" I whispered. "He must *really* like Alex."

Kat and I explored while we waited for the drinks. The beach here was totally different from where we had snorkeled. Rocks and shells lay inches thick. We were taking selfies when Mike called us over.

"Jack called. He should be here in five minutes. He said to go ahead and order."

The margaritas came. They were really good—and really strong. We were diving into some chips and salsa when a tall guy rounded the corner. He wasn't in uniform, but he sure didn't look like a tourist.

"Jackie!" Mike leaped up. He met Jack halfway and gave him a solid handshake.

"Mikey, my friend! It's good to see you!"

Mikey? Jackie? Seriously?

Our food arrived, and as we ate we were entertained with stories from their training. We were all laughing—I couldn't imagine Mike being as crazy as Jack made him out to be.

The talk turned to Jack's work. Mike asked questions. I was surprised that Jack answered them, especially in front of us.

"We still can't figure out exactly what happened in January," Jack said. "It's driving us crazy. We believe the cartels were involved. But we're wondering if someone local was calling the shots. My second-in-command, Roberto, thinks we're getting close to the truth. This rap festival is my big worry now. We don't want a repeat of BPM, the music festival in Playa."

"You've bumped up security?" Mike asked.

Jack nodded. "We brought in an expert from the States. A guy named Eric Cohen. But you never know who's playing both sides."

"Dirty cops?" Mike asked.

Jack nodded. "Some for sure. Which just makes this harder." Jack sipped his drink. "Rob—Roberto—thinks there's one person at the top. Someone local, like I said. If that's true, this person is very good at hiding. In the shadows, pulling the strings." Jack looked intense. "The cartels *do* seem to be pushing into our area. We don't know if our local crooks will fight back. That may be what happened at BPM. Or maybe they will join them. If they haven't already." Jack shrugged. "One thing's for sure. We need to get it under control soon. Nothing stops tourists faster than bad press. And tourism is our life here."

The waiter brought the bill. Jack grabbed it. Mike tried to argue.

"You're my guests," Jack said. "Which reminds me. I want to take you golfing, Mikey. Just nine holes, for old times' sake."

"You're way too busy! And I didn't bring my clubs," Mike said. "Anyway, I'm here with the kids."

"I won't take no for an answer. I need a little downtime, and you have to see this course. It's just south of Cancun. I have an extra set of clubs. It will have to be tomorrow morning though. It's the only time I can get away."

"Go for it, Daddy. Tom and I will be fine on our own at the resort," Kat said.

On our own at the resort.

"Yeah, you should go, Mike," I agreed.

"If it's any help, I wouldn't mind going into Cancun for some shopping. Maybe Kat and Tom want to come with me." Alex looked hopeful. "If you add my name to the car's rental contract, Mike, we could drop you off. Then I could take the kids into Cancun."

All I heard was *shopping*.

That was all Kat heard too.

"Shopping? In Cancun? That sounds great!"

Ugh.

"I don't want to crash your female bonding," I said. "I think I'll stay at the resort."

"I wouldn't want to go either," Mike said, laughing.

"Then it's all settled," Jack said. "I'll call you with the details. And Mike, give the kids my personal cell number." He turned to us. "If you run into any trouble and can't reach your dad, call me. I've got people everywhere in the Mayan." He smiled as he started to walk away. "It was lovely meeting you all. And enjoy yourselves tomorrow. I'm afraid poor Mike won't." Jack was grinning from ear to ear now. "I'm going to kick his ass in golf."

Chapter Ten

It turned out I didn't have to stay at the resort alone. When we got back, there was a message for me from Antonio. Someone had chartered the marina's big yacht for a trip up the coast, but they were short a crewman. If I was willing to wear the uniform, Antonio had permission for me to fill in. Why not? A day on the water, and a chance to see the southern coastline from a new perspective. I couldn't wait.

Early the next morning, Kat, Alex and Mike headed out. I enjoyed sleeping in and having the suite to myself. I called Dad. He made me FaceTime him so he could see the suite.

I met Antonio at twelve thirty and changed into the resort shirt. Then he showed me around the yacht. We were taking four people up the coast to Akumal and back. Antonio's boss would captain, and we would crew. Antonio would double as bartender.

He got me going on prep. I was in the galley, cutting up limes, when I heard voices. Our guests had arrived.

Antonio gave them a tour of the yacht as I cast off. I joined the captain on the bridge when I was done. I couldn't see the men but knew they were outside.

The captain started the motor. I am a true marina kid, and I felt myself relax at the sound. I asked the captain if he needed me to do anything else. He shook his head.

Antonio joined us on the bridge. He spoke to the captain in Spanish. Then he handed me a map.

"I told him to point out what you are seeing. His English is okay. But the map should help." He went back down.

The captain turned out to be a great tour guide. The coast was beautiful. We passed one resort after another. They were all amazing. Between the resorts were villas. Marinas. White-sand beaches. Endless coves and palm trees. And everywhere I looked, boats of all sizes danced on the water.

We were nearing Akumal when the intercom buzzed. "Tom, can you bring me four more *cervezas* from the galley and some extra limes?" Antonio asked.

I found the beers in the galley fridge. I put them on a tray with the limes and balanced it while I opened the glass door to the deck. I handed Antonio the tray and turned.

This was the first chance I'd had to see our guests—and one looked really familiar. It was Red Shirt, the guy from the airport!

My radar was going off like crazy. What were the chances of us running into each other again here?

He recognized me too. He pulled me aside while Antonio refreshed the drinks.

"I've seen you before," Red Shirt said softly. "And I'd love to know what you're doing on this boat." He stared at me intently.

"I'm helping out a friend," I said. "And I think the captain needs me."

I raced back up to the bridge. We were now on our way back to the resort. I couldn't focus. My brain was numb.

What is Red Shirt doing here?

I hadn't seen him since the airport. Sure, he still looked like an ordinary tourist. But his three friends didn't. Two looked like businessmen, not tourists at all. The other looked like he was probably part of the rap fest. He had rings and chains all over him, and he was massive.

Something told me that Red Shirt was not just an ordinary tourist. But maybe it was all in my head. Was I panicking for nothing? I thought of his black bags appearing out of nowhere. Were they why he needed a private driver? I couldn't think straight.

I tried to hear what the group was saying. But with the boat's motor running, it was impossible. I was grateful when the marina came in sight.

When the boat stopped I leaped onto the dock and grabbed the bow line.

Antonio tied down the stern. I got back on the yacht and stayed out of sight on the bridge. Red Shirt and his friends made their way toward the dock from the back of the boat. They stood right under me as Red Shirt spoke quietly.

"So that's it. The whole thing's covered. Everyone just needs to do his job." I could see the other three nodding. "We'll have no trouble pulling this off. But everyone needs to stick to my plan."

Pulling off what?

My mind was spinning. I replayed the words in my head again. It really did sound bad.

Could Red Shirt be part of the cartel?

My cell phone started to ping. There had been no service out on the water. Now my messages were rolling in. Two more dings followed while I dug my phone out of my pocket.

The texts were from Kat. When I saw them, I forgot everything else.

Tom! Are you there?

Call me

Daddy's been shot!

Chapter Eleven

I rushed to call Kat. My hands were shaking.

Let Mike be okay.

Kat had already lost her mom.

Why wasn't I with her?

Where was Alex? And Jack?

Kat picked up. "Oh, Tom! Thank god!" She started crying. "I'm so glad to hear your voice."

"How's Mike? Is he going to be okay? What happened?" I couldn't help firing questions at her. "How are you? Are you okay?"

"Daddy's alive. He just came out of surgery. I haven't seen him yet. We're waiting to talk to the doctor," Kat said. "Alex is with me."

"Is Jack there?"

"No, because he got a call. Another awful thing happened. He thinks they're connected."

"What other thing?"

"Do you remember Jack talking about his second-in-command, Roberto?"

"Yeah." I felt my stomach sink. "Did they shoot him too?"

"No. But this morning his little girl was kidnapped!" I could hear Kat taking a deep breath. "Jack thinks the cartels did it. And he thinks they shot Daddy by mistake when they were aiming for him. He feels terrible."

"Are there any leads?"

"No one's claimed anything yet. But Jack thinks they wanted both him and Rob out of the way."

"So something big must be happening soon. That rap fest starts tonight." My mind spun. "Well, they didn't get Jack. And I'm sure he's all over it. But Rob must be going out of his mind."

"I know. Can you imagine? Amelia is only eight!" Kat said. "It's been all over the news. Her driver was dropping her off late at school. Two men beat him up. They grabbed her. No one has seen her since."

"I'll come into Cancun. I can grab a cab."

"No, stay there. As much as I want you here, there's nothing you can do. Alex is keeping me company." I heard Alex say hi in the background. "And Jack will be back at some point." She took

Martha Brack Martin

another big breath. "You hold down the fort. I'll call you once I know more. You should call your dad though."

My dad. He was going to flip.

"Okay. But call me the minute you know something. And if you change your mind, I'll be there in a flash."

"I will. I don't know what I'd do without you, Tom. Thanks for being here."

"I'm just a phone call away. Now go take care of your dad."

Antonio had heard my end of the call. He saw that I was shaken and offered to clean up the yacht by himself. I headed back to our suite.

Sure enough, the English newscast was reporting both stories. They didn't give many details about Mike's shooting, but they showed pictures of Amelia in her school uniform. She was all braids and a big smile. I kept the news on and called Dad.

He freaked out. No surprise.

"I'll let our contacts here know," Dad said. "You keep your head down and take care of Kat. And text me when you know anything more."

I grabbed dinner at the buffet. For once I didn't care what I was eating. Then I went back to the suite to charge my phone. Kat called later with good news.

"The doctor says he's going to be okay." I could hear the relief in her voice. "He's not awake yet. But that's all that matters."

Mike was going to make it. I felt like I could breathe again.

"I'm going to stay here tonight," Kat said. "I want to be here when he wakes up. Alex is staying too. We'll be fine."

I texted Dad the good news. I felt too wired to sleep, so I headed out for a walk. The resort was still partying hard. I kept walking and found myself at the marina. It was quiet at this time of night, the boats floating peacefully. It felt like home.

When I'd read Kat's texts about Mike, I'd forgotten all about Red Shirt. But now, seeing the yacht again, I remembered.

What was the plan Red Shirt had talked about? Was he part of whatever was going on?

My head was pounding. So many crazy things were happening at the same time. Red Shirt showing up. Mike getting shot. Rob's little girl being kidnapped. Even the rap fest starting. Maybe they really *were* all connected. Dad always says there's no such thing as coincidence. My radar was on overload.

The silence was suddenly broken. I heard Spanish voices drifting over the water. I could see two men sitting on the deck of a sailboat docked in one of the last slips. I hadn't noticed it before, so it must have come in recently.

The boat was a real beauty. A forty-footer at least. Worth big money.

I moved closer to get a better look at the men. The marina lights were dimmed at this time of night. I kept to the shadows.

One of the men had long hair and was in a bathing suit. The other had a big beard. He was wrapped in a towel. Even in the low light, both men looked rough. Long Hair passed a joint to Big Beard. They didn't look like they could afford a boat like that—though who was I to judge? Still, I had grown up at a marina. I was familiar with all the "types." Maybe they were security, but they sure didn't look it.

I gave my head—and my radar—a shake. It was getting late. Instead of seeing bad guys everywhere, I needed to get some sleep. The next day would probably be a long one.

Hopefully there'd be no more surprises.

Chapter Twelve

My phone woke me up. Kat had finally seen her dad. Mike was pretty out of it. They'd loaded him up with painkillers.

"He couldn't talk, but he tried to push the pills away. Typical Daddy." Kat sounded better. "Jack called too. He's busy, but he wanted to check in. He asked if Daddy could tell him what happened yet, but I told him no."

"I'm glad he's coming around. I'll get the local bus and head to Cancun after breakfast. I miss you."

"I miss you too. But you might as well stay there. Alex and I will be bringing the rental car back soon. We're just waiting for Daddy to wake up a bit more."

"Oh. Okay. Well, tell Mike I said hi. And let him know I called my dad," I said. "Text me when you're on your way back. And drive safely." I almost told Kat about Red Shirt but decided she had enough on her mind.

I took my time over breakfast. I read the resort issue of *USA Today*. There was a story in it about the Rap in the Riv Fest. The story quoted Eric Cohen, the security expert Jack had mentioned.

It was crazy how fast things could change in a few days. One minute we were having a dream vacation. Snorkeling. Kissing. The next minute,

Mike was in the hospital, a little girl had been kidnapped, and everyone seemed shady.

Thinking about shady reminded me about the sailboat I'd seen the night before. Since I was killing time until Kat got back anyway, I decided I would go and take another look.

The sailboat was still in its slip. I was pretty sure it was a Tartan. Worth $300,000 at least. Only Long Hair was on deck. He was playing on his phone.

Maybe Big Beard was inside. I scanned the boat's windows.

Nothing.

Maybe he was lying down.

Suddenly a face popped up in the biggest window. Definitely not Big Beard's. A little girl's face, pale and surrounded by long braids. I recognized it from the TV news the night before.

Amelia.

Am I going crazy?

I looked closer. Nope. Same school uniform. Same braids. There was no question about it. Rob's little girl was on that boat!

As my mind tried to process it, I watched Amelia waving her arms back and forth. I didn't think she could see me, but she was clearly trying to get noticed.

I grabbed my phone. I needed to whisper, since sound carries over water and Long Hair was still on deck.

"Kat! You're never going to believe this! Roberto's daughter is here. On a sailboat in the resort marina."

Kat was Kat. Now that she knew Mike was going to be okay, she was calm again. "*Amelia?* Is she safe? Can you get to her?"

"There's at least one guard. Maybe two. Ask your dad what I should do."

"Daddy's still groggy. Call Jack."

"Okay."

"Call your dad too. And promise me you won't do anything stupid. I'm not beside you this time." She hung up.

I called Dad, but he didn't answer. I left him a long message. Then I tried to call Jack. He didn't pick up either. I asked him to call me. I didn't leave details in case one of the crooked cops had tapped his phone.

Long Hair went into the cabin. Amelia's face disappeared. I watched and waited, feeling useless. My phone was set to vibrate, but no one called.

It seemed like forever before Long Hair came back up. He jumped off the boat. Then he headed to the parking lot. He never looked back once. That made me nervous.

There was no one else around the marina and still no sign of Big Beard. Long Hair was gone—at least, for now. This was my best chance to get Amelia out of there. I just needed time.

I walked to the slip and climbed onto the boat. The cabin door was unlocked. I wondered why—until I saw Amelia.

She was tied up and gagged. Her eyes went wide when she saw me.

I smiled at her, but I didn't waste time talking. I grabbed a knife from the galley and cut her free. Then I used the knife to cut the fuel line—I didn't want these losers getting away once they realized Amelia was gone. I grabbed a ballcap from the counter and tucked Amelia's braids under it.

"Now we go," I said. "*Vamos!*" Amelia nodded.

We crept to the deck. No sign of Long Hair. Amelia held my hand tightly as we leaped off the boat and raced down the dock. On shore, I slowed to a walk. We needed to blend in. Not that her school uniform made that easy. I grabbed the first beach towel I saw and wrapped it around her.

I tried not to look over my shoulder. I didn't relax until we were back in the suite.

"It's okay. You're safe," I said. "I'm Tom." I pointed at myself.

Though she hadn't said a word before now, Amelia suddenly starting speaking Spanish a mile a minute. I shook my head. She pointed to the bathroom. *That* I understood. She went in and closed the door behind her. I called Kat.

"I tell you not to take risks. Then you go rescue her all by yourself?" Kat tried to sound mad, but I could tell she was proud. "Call Jack again. We can't trust anyone else. The cartels probably have people in the resort. Maybe that's why they picked that marina," Kat said.

I thought of Antonio and his boss. I was sure they were honest.

Kat was still talking. "You'd better stay hidden until Jack gets there. Alex is grabbing a coffee. My Spanish isn't great, but let me try talking to Amelia. Maybe she can tell us more."

Amelia walked out of the bathroom. I handed her my phone.

"Papa?" Her face fell when she heard Kat's voice. But then I could see her starting to relax. Soon she was talking to Kat like an old friend. Finally Amelia nodded. "*Gracias*," she said, handing me the phone.

Kat filled me in. "I told her she's safe with us. She wanted to call her dad. I told her the bad guys might be listening. She understood. She's a bright kid." I was impressed by how much Kat had learned. "She seems pretty tough. They didn't feed her, so she's hungry. Can you find her some food? And she needs to get out of that school uniform. I told her she could borrow some of my clothes. See if you can find something small enough."

"I'm so glad you learned Spanish in school," I said. Kat laughed as she hung up.

Amelia needed food, but room service was our only option—I wasn't about to leave her alone or take her outside. I ordered some things I thought Amelia would like, as well as a coffee for me, while she went into the bedroom to look through Kat's clothes.

My cell phone vibrated. *Jack.*

Finally!

I told him everything. He was amazed I'd found Amelia. Even more shocked that I'd gotten her off the boat. At least he didn't lecture me. I'd get enough of that from Dad.

"You were right to call. I'll come to the resort and get you. That's the safest plan. Don't trust anyone, and stay put."

"Okay," I promised. "We'll wait in the suite until you get here." I gave him the room and building numbers.

"I will be there as soon as I can," he said.

The food arrived. After the server was gone, Amelia came out of the bedroom, wearing one of Kat's T-shirts. It hung on her like a dress, but at least she looked a little different. I handed her the ballcap from the boat, and she tucked up her braids again.

Amelia dove into her food. I took my coffee and went out to the balcony. I figured I'd watch for Jack. Try to breathe a little and calm down.

I looked around as I took a sip.

And then I almost choked.

Long Hair and Big Beard were walking through the resort.

They'd cleaned up, but there was no mistaking them. They were walking quickly. Like they knew exactly where they were going.

I was pretty sure I knew where they were going too.

They were heading straight for our building.

They were coming for us.

Chapter Thirteen

I ran back into the suite. Amelia read the panic on my face.

"Tom?" My name sounded like a cry on her lips.

"We have to go! *Vamos*." I ran around the room, grabbing my wallet, my phone, my charger. Even my passport. "Fast!" Amelia nodded. Fear is a language everybody knows.

We raced out the door. The men had been walking toward the front of our building. We took the back stairs.

I didn't wait to see if we were followed. We flew down the path behind the buildings. Jack might have arrived by now. Making our way to the lobby seemed like the best plan.

The room-service guy must be in on it. Or maybe they saw me at the marina after all and then spotted me on the balcony.

I looked at Amelia. She gave me a shaky smile. She was scared, but she kept moving.

The path led us around the lobby to the resort entrance. We stopped and hid.

A couple of cabs were waiting. A van unloaded new guests. Behind them, a tour bus idled. There was no sign of Jack.

We couldn't afford to wait. The guys chasing us could catch up to us any second. I looked at the tour bus. People were starting to get on.

"We're leaving," I said, pointing at the bus. I took Amelia's hand. Hopefully everyone would assume she was my little sister.

I thought they'd ask my name, but they just wanted my money. I paid, and the bus pulled away as we sat down. I took a quick peek at the lobby. No bad guys in sight. But no Jack either.

The bus was heading to the Tulum ruins. *Kat will be jealous I'm seeing some ruins before she is.* I didn't want anyone on the bus to hear me, so I texted Jack instead of calling him.

Bad guys showed up

Had to run

Now on bus to Tulum ruins

Jack texted back:

Don't talk to anyone.

Big ears everywhere.

I will meet you there.

I texted Kat next. I gave her the short version, that Amelia was safe, that we were on our way to Tulum, that I'd fill her in later. She told me they'd taken Mike for tests and he'd been gone for almost an hour. He was still out of it. She didn't want to leave without telling him what was up. She was a lot more freaked out now, though, knowing that the bad guys were actually after us.

It was a long ride. Amelia dozed off while I was texting. I googled the ruins. I needed to find a safe place where we could wait for Jack. Somewhere the bad guys wouldn't find us first.

Then Kat texted again:

Daddy's back

He's awake

Thank god. I wondered if it was a good idea for her to go back to the resort in case there were other bad guys hanging around. I was about to reply when another text came.

Then another.

I had to read them twice. I couldn't wrap my head around them.

Daddy says Jack is dirty!

Don't trust him!

There was a brief pause. Then one final text came through:

Run!!

Chapter Fourteen

Run? Run where?

The ruins were just ahead. I shook Amelia awake. She darted into the bus bathroom. While she was gone I tried to think.

Jack was a dirty cop.

He could be right behind us. His goons too. Now I knew how they'd found us so fast. He'd told them exactly where we were.

We needed a place to hide. But I didn't know the Tulum ruins. I needed someone who knew this area. Someone I could trust.

Antonio!

I texted him as fast as I could. I didn't wait for a reply.

It's Tom

I'm in trouble

I found Amelia

Kidnapped girl

She's with me

Bad guys r after us @Tulum ruins

Need to hide

Can u help?

I held my breath until he replied:

Yes

Try to get to beach

Go thru ruins

Our bus unloaded. Amelia and I joined the crowd. We got on a trolley that dropped us off at the entrance.

Poor Amelia had no idea what was going on. I couldn't understand her, and she couldn't understand me. I didn't dare call Kat and have someone overhear me. But I needed a translator.

Then it hit me. I pulled out my phone.

Gotta love Google.

I opened Google Translate. I wrote that her dad's boss was coming after us. We had thought he was a good guy, but he wasn't. We needed a place to hide.

Amelia grabbed my phone and read it. She typed a reply and Google translated it.

I call my Papa, I read. *He help.*

I nodded. It was time we called him anyway. Jack was the one who had told us not to contact Roberto.

Amelia started to cry when she heard her dad's voice, but she recovered fast. She spoke quietly. I didn't understand anything she said. But by the time she hung up, we were on the move.

This time *she* grabbed *my* hand. She took me back to the market by the parking lot. I was sure we'd run into Jack coming the other way. Somehow we didn't. We wove through the market's stalls and pathways. Amelia was looking for something. She stopped near the back of the market, at stall twenty-three. She motioned me in.

An old Mayan man sat on a stool. He was surrounded by blankets. Piles of them covered the floor. A table with more stood behind him. He got up when we walked in and spoke Spanish very quickly. Amelia replied just as rapidly, nodding. He made room for us to sit on the floor, half hidden. Then he left.

Amelia still had my phone. She typed fast.

This is a man who gives my Papa information. Papa told him we would come. He hides us.

I nodded. An informant. I wondered if he knew that Jack was dirty.

I updated Kat.

Amelia called her dad

We r hiding in market by ruins

Stall 23

She answered:

We r coming

Stay safe

When my phone shook again, I thought it was Kat. I had a moment of panic when I saw it was from Jack.

Where are you? I'm at the parking lot.
So close!

I needed to send Jack far away.

We r behind biggest temple

Hopefully that would buy us a bit of time.

The stall owner walked back in. He handed us tacos and drinks. The icy lemonade was perfect. It was hotter than an oven in the stall.

We'd finished eating when Jack texted again.

I can't find you. Are you okay?

I didn't know what to reply. A few minutes passed. Then he texted again.

Have you heard from Kat?

He must be wondering if Mike had woken up and we were all onto him. I couldn't answer.

Hopefully he'll think my battery died.

I looked at Amelia. She was fading fast in this heat. I opened a game app on my phone. She was happy to play. Distracting myself was harder.

After a while she handed back my phone. Now the battery *was* almost dead.

I needed a quick stretch. I stood up just as the stall owner turned toward the doorway. He must have heard something I didn't.

POP!

I turned at the sudden noise. Everything seemed to happen in slow motion.

The stall owner slid to the floor at my feet. I saw a fresh bullet hole right in the middle of his forehead. His eyes stared up at me blankly. Amelia began to scream.

Then Jack stepped into the stall.

In his right hand was a gun with a silencer. He grabbed Amelia with his left and covered her mouth in one smooth motion.

He looked at me. And then he smiled.

"*Hola*, Tom," he said.

Chapter Fifteen

The two guys from the sailboat were right behind Jack. Long Hair grabbed Amelia and said something to her in Spanish. She didn't try to scream anymore. Instead she kept her eyes on Jack's gun. She looked terrified.

Big Beard dragged the dead stall owner under the table. He threw a blanket over him. Jack said something and the two goons left. Amelia stood there frozen.

"You may as well sit," he said to me. "And I'll take your phone." I handed it over. "We need to wait for a bit. There are too many people right now."

Too many for what? I was afraid to ask.

"It seems you've learned about my other job. When I couldn't find you, I wondered. Then you didn't answer. I knew where you must be." Jack pointed under the table. "I know all about our informants and where to find them. That's why I'm the boss." He shrugged. "Only Roberto could have led you here."

Amelia looked up at her father's name.

"So now I *know* you have talked to him. No matter. I knew I would have to kill him eventually. But I was hoping to delay a bit longer. Plan an accident."

He shrugged. "Oh well. My men have gone to arrange it now."

I looked at Amelia. She was shaking. Thank goodness she didn't understand English.

"Rob has suspected me for some time," Jack went on. "That's why I took Amelia. I needed to keep him busy. And then she would become insurance if he tried to come after me. I only needed a couple of days."

I wondered where Kat and Alex were. Was Rob walking into a trap? Jack's two goons were out there somewhere. What if they saw Kat and hurt her too?

I felt sick knowing there was nothing I could do about any of it.

"I'm making history, you know," Jack said proudly. "The big cartels *never* work together. Not if they can help it. But now they want to come here. And to 'play' in the Mayan, they will have to do things my way." He sounded smug. "It will be better for everyone. No more shootings in high-tourist areas. No more drawing attention to themselves, advertising their activities. Too sloppy." He shook his head. "They need a single leader. One who knows how we do things *here*. I'm meeting with my new business partners tomorrow night. Not as myself, of course. They can't know who I really am. Only Rob has figured it out so far." He paused. "And my old friend Mike."

I tried not to react, but Jack noticed.

"Ah, I thought so." Jack nodded. "That's too bad. I was afraid Mike had put it all together. He's too good an agent. That's why I needed him out of the way."

"So you shot him?"

"No, my new partners did. That's the secret, you see. All the dirty work is done by the cartels. I keep my hands clean. They don't even know a Maya is giving them orders."

"If you knew Mike was that smart, why did you hide Amelia at *our* resort? There are other marinas."

"I'd already put things in place before I knew Mike was coming here. I needed a marina open to the public. Not too busy. And I wanted one where none of my own people worked, so no one could identify me."

"Well, I found her," I said, "so your planning sucked."

Jack laughed. "Ah, but you didn't connect her to me. Though I give you credit. Who knew a teenager could stage a solo rescue operation?" He paused. "And now here we are."

He looked at his watch. We'd been here for hours. It had to be after five. I realized the busy sounds of the crowd wandering through the market were gone.

"And now you and Amelia are standing in my way." Amelia looked up again at hearing her name. "She will go back with my men to the marina. This time they'll do a better job. Once my meetings are finished, I'll find and 'rescue' her. Sadly, it will be too late. She'll die in the takedown. As will my men, although they don't know that part. But they've seen the real me. And I can't afford any witnesses."

"You've got it all figured out, don't you?"

"I told you. I'm good at what I do." He shrugged. "*You* I will have to take care of tonight. We're all going to the beach here. We've got a boat waiting. By now the swimmers will be gone."

"Are you planning to shoot me?" I was surprised I got the words out.

"Oh no. We don't need more news like that. Tourists who get shot make the news. Take Mike, for example."

He walked toward the stall opening, keeping one eye on me. He briefly checked outside. "I'm afraid you're going to drown. Poor Kat will be so sad. Especially after losing her dad." Jack smiled at the look on my face. "Oh yes, my new partners will arrange for Mike to have an unexpected setback. Losing both you and her dad will be too much for Kat. She will probably end up hurting herself." He grinned again. "All my loose ends tied up. I told you—I can't have any witnesses."

I wanted to punch him in the head. Could I manage it before he shot me?

"Sadly, some people are too curious." He pointed at the blanket covering the stall owner's body. "This is what happens when you don't mind your own business. It's never a happy ending. Just ask him."

Chapter Sixteen

Jack pulled out his phone and spoke to someone. He didn't take his eyes off us. Then the two goons came back. Jack put his gun in his holster. His shirt covered it.

"Now you're going to experience one of the most famous beaches in the Mayan area. Sadly, you won't enjoy it for long." He led us out of the market.

Big Beard and Long Hair flanked us. There was no way Amelia or I could make a run for it.

We walked through the market to the ruins. The area was almost empty. I scanned our surroundings as we walked, and I could see Amelia doing the same. The whole place was breathtaking—but I didn't care. The only sight I wanted to see was Kat. Preferably escorted by an army of cops.

Jack stopped at the top of a flight of steps that led to the beach.

"Don't try anything on these stairs. You'll just be saving me trouble." The stairs were wooden and slippery. I grabbed the railing. So did Amelia.

The beach was empty. Just a jet ski parked on the sand and a snorkeling boat a few yards offshore. It looked like we were on our own.

As we got near the bottom, Long Hair went ahead. He climbed on the jet ski and motored to the boat in seconds. He tied the jet ski to the stern. Slowly he lifted anchor and trolled into shore.

"Get going." Jack motioned toward the boat. I picked up Amelia and carried her through the shallow water. Jack and Big Beard followed.

As soon as we were all seated, Jack took out his gun again. Then he said something in Spanish. Long Hair untied the jet ski and got on. In seconds he was around the rocks to the north and out of sight.

Big Beard started up the motor.

I put on a life jacket and gave one to Amelia. I was pretty sure it wouldn't help me survive what Jack had planned. But using one was habit.

I reached for Amelia's hand. She took mine in a death grip. We both searched the shoreline. Nothing.

Big Beard pointed the boat north. We wove around fish boats floating nearby.

A few diving and tour boats were out too. I thought about signaling them. But how?

Big Beard was looking around. He said something to Jack. I saw Amelia look up, studying the boats we were passing. Jack shrugged.

I looked more closely at the boats. One was heading in the same direction as us. It was bright green. When it cut across our wake, I saw its name—*The Thirsty Turtle.*

Antonio's grandfather's boat!

Suddenly our boat lurched.

Jack barked at Big Beard in Spanish. Big Beard said something back.

Our motor started sputtering. Then the boat lurched again. I didn't need to know Spanish to see Big Beard had no idea why the motor was acting up.

Jack swore and yelled. It was nice to see him losing his cool.

The motor coughed a couple more times.

Then it died altogether.

I didn't grow up around a marina for nothing. I knew there was no way that motor had died all by itself. Someone had tampered with it before we boarded. I looked around for *The Thirsty Turtle*. It was still coming up behind us.

Clearly, we weren't alone after all.

Jack was still yelling and swearing. Big Beard kept trying the motor. Neither of them was paying attention to anything else.

All the boats in the area were slowly turning in our direction. *The Thirsty Turtle* was close enough for me to see Antonio at the wheel.

Things were about to get wild. I could feel it. Help was close—but we needed to put some space between us and Jack.

I wrapped an arm around Amelia. Without a word, I tipped us both over the side, snorkel style.

Amelia coughed up some water—but she was okay. We floated near the boat, staying close to the starboard side near the bow, out of Jack's sight line.

The Thirsty Turtle was only a few yards away now. Antonio must have gone full throttle when he saw us go over the side. A tall man in uniform and a trio of soldiers were pointing long rifles at Jack and Big Beard from the *Turtle's* deck.

The tall man yelled something in Spanish. All I recognized was "Joaquin." Amelia listened closely. Jack yelled something from our boat. I saw Amelia smile.

There was a sudden flurry of activity as boats closed in around us. The officers boarded our boat and took control.

Now that Jack wasn't a threat, Amelia and I swam over to the *Turtle* and climbed aboard. Antonio welcomed us with a huge grin.

"Antonio! How did you do this?" I asked. "The motor, the soldiers? All these boats?"

"I told you. Abuelo knows everyone. You texted me. I called him." Antonio waved at the shoreline. A white-haired man was coming down the cliffs. He waved back. "He was happy to help with their boat—and he brought some friends." Antonio gestured at all the boats. "Normally there would not be all these boats out here."

That must have been what Big Beard noticed.

"You had some help of your own too." Antonio pointed to a big yacht racing toward us. I could see Kat waving on deck. Beside her were uniformed officers and two men in regular clothes.

"PAPA!" Amelia shrieked.

I realized I knew one of the men too—even though I couldn't believe

I was seeing him. I pointed at the second man. "And that's *my* papa," I said.

Antonio said he needed to go get his abuelo from the beach. I thanked him again and promised we'd catch up back at the resort. *The Thirsty Turtle* took off as soon as we boarded the police boat.

I didn't know who to hug first. Kat decided for me. She wrapped her arms around me and kissed me until I couldn't breathe.

"Okay, enough of that," Dad said, pulling me into a big hug. We were both a little choked up.

"How did you get here?" I asked. My dad never left home, unless it was to see a Tigers game in Detroit. And he hadn't done that in years.

"You needed me. You think I wasn't going to come and make sure you were all okay?" His look included Kat.

"Dangerous shit was happening. The second we hung up, I called the airport. Got a ticket on the first plane to Cancun." He let out a shaky breath and looked at Kat. "Even then we barely made it in time."

I pictured the dead informant on the floor of his stall. "Not in time for everyone."

I thought of Jack, cuffed and loaded on a smaller police boat coming behind us. Jail was too good for him.

"Well, it could have been worse. Mike was able to warn you about Jack," Dad said. "And you saved that little girl's life," he added, pointing.

Amelia and Rob walked over to us. Amelia gave me a big hug. Then Rob gave me one too.

"I cannot thank you enough, Tom," he said. He had tears in his eyes. "You found my girl and kept her safe."

"She's very tough—and very brave."

Rob translated for Amelia, who grinned. "She gets that from her mama," he said.

"I'm glad you're okay too, sir," I said. "Jack told me he'd ordered a hit on you. One of his goons took off on a jet ski to set it up."

"We picked him up on our way here. He was happy to talk," Rob said. "My men in Cancun picked up my would-be killers. We have also taken into custody the two men who were planning to hurt Kat's father."

"So Mike's safe? Are you sure?"

"He's fine," Kat said. "Your dad made it to the hospital just as Alex and I were leaving. Alex stayed with Daddy. I texted her a few minutes ago to say you're okay. Daddy's good. And they aren't alone anyway. Your dad made sure some of their 'friends' stayed in the hospital to guard him."

I looked at Dad. "Friends?"

"I got permission for a few of Mike's agents to meet me in Cancun. We pulled a few strings. And as great as Alex seemed, I wasn't leaving Mike alone with her. For all I knew, she could have worked for Jack. With all this crazy double-crossing stuff, I wasn't taking any chances. But it turns out she's just a nice lady from Virginia after all."

I had to laugh. Like father, like son. No wonder my radar was always on high alert.

"Mike's buddies were allowed to come," Dad continued. "But we *did* get stopped at Immigration. Seems passports of people in their line of work are getting some extra attention right now."

I thought of Mike getting pulled in at the Cancun airport. They must have flagged his passport too.

"I'm afraid you have me to blame for that." The voice came from behind

Kat and Dad. They moved aside to make
room for the speaker. When I saw who it
was, I couldn't believe it.

Red Shirt.

Rob was smiling. "This is Eric
Cohen, the security expert we brought
in from the States," he said. "I hear you
met him already."

Red Shirt was Eric Cohen, the guy
I'd read about in the paper? My brain
was spinning again.

"So your meeting on the marina
yacht was about security?" I asked.

Red Shirt—Eric—looked surprised.
"So you *did* hear us?"

"Not really. I thought maybe you
were with the cartels. You talked
about your plans—" I stopped, feeling
stupid.

"You really aren't a regular kid,
are you?" Eric sounded impressed. "If
you ever want a job, come see me. I'm

based in Detroit." He turned to Rob. "In the meantime, I need to get going."

"Jack's meeting with the cartels is going ahead tomorrow night. Since he kept his real identity secret, we have someone taking his place," Rob explained. "With luck, we will be able to grab the leaders of the cartels at the meeting. The word *Cancun* actually means 'the nest of the snakes.' Hopefully we will cut off a few snakes' heads tomorrow night. And then we can drive the cartels out of the Mayan Riviera." Rob looked at Amelia. "But tonight we'll just have a quiet evening at home."

Amelia hugged me again. Then she and her dad went below.

"We're getting dropped off at the resort," Dad explained. "I can't wait to see that suite in person. And that marina!" He grinned like a kid. "How late are the

bars open? I could really use a drink."
With that, Dad wandered below, probably
looking for one.

"We've created a vacation monster,"
I said.

"That's okay. Then he'll want to
come back here again." Kat wrapped her
arms around me. She put her head on
my shoulder. "After the last two days, I
feel like I need a whole new vacation."

I nodded. "Me too. At least we have
tomorrow. And they'll need us back to
testify as some point, I guess."

"True. Daddy's talked them into
letting him out of the hospital first thing
tomorrow. I tried to argue. But you
know what he's like."

"Well then. Here's to one more full
day for now. We're all safe. And we'll
all be together soon," I said. "Most
importantly, I'm with you. As lame as it
sounds, that's my definition of paradise."

"Back at you."

Then Kat gave me a very long, very hot kiss.

Paradise was looking up.

Acknowledgments

Any good teacher-librarian will tell you that research is important. I was very blessed to have some great research companions helping me out with *Mayan Murder* and its prequel, *River Traffic*.

My boating and marina enthusiasts: Cynthia Goddard, Alexander Mickle, the Mancinis, Terri Patterson, Rob Ferguson and Rob Wilkie.

My Detroit River experts: Rob Ferguson, Vicki Petras and the Pattersons.

My law-enforcement connections: Michael Martin and Joe Rafuse.

My on-site research team for *River Traffic*: Laura and Meaghan Wilkie, Emma Martin and Sophie the Smiling Research Dog.

My on-site research partners: the Schauer family and Carol Legge, who have been our frequent companions in the Mayan—and who witnessed the flabongo firsthand!

I've also been blessed to have some fabulous writer buddies I'd like to thank:

Marsha Skrypuch, who took my writing interest and turned it into a passion. Thanks, Sensei, for everything—from Kidcrit to Book Camp to contract help.

Eric Walters, who kept encouraging me to start writing again and then let me do it in my own way, in my own time. (You were right—Andrew is a "good guy.")

Julie Kentner, who leaped into the breach to edit. We'll always have Sir Henry and the Ho Inn.

Marina Cohen, who has never stopped being my cheerleader, beta reader, plot prodder and confidante. Thanks for sharing the journey with me and never losing faith that I'd be joining you on a fiction shelf someday! This book is especially for you.

Last but not least, I'd like to thank Andrew Wooldridge and the Orca pod for welcoming me with open dorsal fins and showing me how to navigate the shoals of fiction publishing. You guys rock!

Martha Brack Martin is the author of the Orca Soundings title *River Traffic*, which was chosen as a Best Bets for Kids and Teens 2017 by the Canadian Children's Book Centre. She is also an award-winning teacher–librarian. She lives in a small town near Windsor, Ontario.

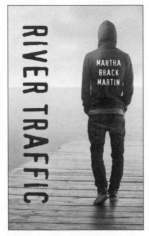

RIVER TRAFFIC

MARTHA
BRACK
MARTIN

TOM LeFAVE is trying to hold his world together. His family's marina is struggling. His dad is full of secrets. And the quarterback of the football team hates his guts. When a huge yacht docks at Tom's marina, things look brighter, especially when he meets Kat, the daughter of the boat's owner. Kat and Tom share a love of rum-running history. It's not long, however, before Tom starts to realize there's something more than history happening on the river. And if Tom can't figure it out in time, he just might be history too.